Other books by Euftis Emery

Off the Chain

Off the Chain Volume 2

So you want me to do what???

Revenge – Between my Lover's Legs…

I'm Shy…

Published by Dominion Publishing

All rights reserved.

No part of this book may be reproduced in any form or by any electronic or mechanical means including information storage and retrieval systems without written permission from the publisher and or authors, except by reviewers who may quote brief passages.

Review passages may not exceed one column inch or forty-five words excluding articles, whichever is greater.

© 2010, Euftis Emery

Cover design by Euftis Emery; cover model Hotnette; interior model Kaleigh

Editing by Euftis.

Euftis_Emery@yahoo.com

License Notes

This book is licensed for your personal enjoyment only. This book may not be re-sold or given away to other people. If you would like to share this book with another person, please purchase an additional copy for each person you share it with. If you're reading this book and did not purchase it, or it was not purchased for your use only, then you should purchase your own copy. Thank you for respecting the hard work of this author.

Euftis Emery

I'm Shy…

Introduction

This is a story from my upcoming anthology Off the Chain Volume 3. I'll put out each short story individually as I write the anthology. So, you can purchase the individual stories that you like in eBook and pocketsize edition or wait and get OTC Volume 3.

If you enjoy my work, please write a review for me on the website where you purchased my book. If you buy my work from Amazon, I'd also appreciate it if you would post a picture of yourself with the book and tag it.

Euftis Emery

I'm Shy…

I'm shy…
I was in Columbus, Ohio visiting with Pumpkin. She had moved into a condo near Easton Mall and decided to have a little get together with her closest friends to break the place in.

It was getting late and everyone had cleared out with the exception of me and Don, Pumpkin's boyfriend. Pumpkin was so kind to let me stay over for the evening since I lived in Cincinnati and I killed time by chatting with friends on Yahoo Messenger.

"You alright in there", Pumpkin asked as she cleaned up her kitchen. She refrained from calling me…*Daddy*…since her man was around.

"I'm good baby", I replied.

"You want a beer E", Don asked as he pulled a cold one out of the refrigerator.

"What you got", I asked.

"Grolsch and Budweiser", Don replied.

"Grolsch and Budweiser", I exclaimed surprised.
"Now…that's a combination of beer to have in a refrigerator. Pumpkin…what you know about Grolsch", I yelled at her as she continued to wash dishes in the kitchen.

"'Chelle don't know nothin' 'bout beer E", Don replied with a snort. "It's all mine. I got into drinkin' Grolsch while I was

I'm Shy...

in Germany with the Army."

"That's what's up! I'll take a Grolsch man", I replied enthusiastically.
Don took two beers out of the fridge and then walked into the living room where I sat and handed me one. We both popped the signature re-sealable tops on our beers and took a deep swig in unison.

"An ice cold Grolsch is…", I replied with a momentary loss for words.

"I know", Don said with the same satisfied look on his face as me. "I'll drink a Bud every now and then to spread out my beer budget…but this here Grolsch…it's what's up! What you doin'", Don asked curious as he got a glimpse of my laptop monitor.

"I'm chatting with three females on Yahoo", I replied.

"Chatting…", Don replied confused. "You're talkin' to three different women at the same time? Are they friends or somethin'?"

"It's just text baby", Pumpkin explained to Don interrupting as she came out of the kitchen and into the living room. "They are typing to each other."

Don walked up to me and bent over to get a close look at the screen so he could read the conversations. "He's talkin' about hookin' up with one. Gettin' some head from another one. And they ain't gettin' mad at you?"

"He don't have his cam on so they don't know he's talkin' to

Euftis Emery

somebody else at the same time. That's some ultimate playa shit right there", Pumpkin said laughing.

"You got a camera on here to", Don said amazed. "They can see you. Can you see them to?"

"Yea…if they have a cam, I can see them as well", I replied a little amused with Don's Internet naivety.

"Don's not up on all this", Pumpkin cut in. "I set us up a profile on SwingLifeSyle.Com because my baby wants' to start doin' some couple swapping and we are looking for some new friends over there.

We don't have a pic on our profile, so we haven't gotten many hits. I done told Don that if we put some pics on there, we'd get a lot more hits and we can qualify couples that are interested in us by chattin' with them and doing some things on cam. Show him some things Daddy", Pumpkin asked slipping up calling me by my pet name in front of her man.

Luckily, Don was too busy scrolling through the multiple nasty conversations that I was having and didn't hear her. I asked Don to take a step back and then asked one of the women I was chatting with to turn on her camera.

Chayne's camera came to life on my display and an image of her sitting on her bed appeared on a small window. "Who's that", Pumpkin asked getting all up in my business as usual.

"That's my friend Chayne. She lives in St. Louis", I stated.

"So…we are looking at what's she's doin? Right now,", Don

I'm Shy…

asked amazed.

"Yea…we are…", I replied amused as Don shuffled and fidgeted as a new door of sexuality opened before him.

"I don't believe this…", Don stated as he rubbed his head and fidgeted at a faster pace.

"What's…not to believe", Pumpkin exclaimed. "Daddy's friend is on her cam…right there!"

"Daddy", Don questioned raising an eyebrow.

"No disrespect baby", Pumpkin followed up quickly. "That's just my nickname for Euftis."

"I ain't trippin'. I know you and E got this quasi-incestuous brother/sister thing goin' on", Don replied brushing off Pumpkin's comment.

"Now if she's really live on her camera…then make her…*do*…something", Don said still not believing the situation.

"*Let me see those big tits*", I typed in Chayne's message box. Compliant, Chayne immediately pulled her luscious 40" FF's out of her bra and started playing with them.

"I…*don't*…believe this", Don said again as he appeared even more agitated and put both of his hands in his Afro. "Make her do something else."

"Damn those big, soft tits look tasty. Wish I was there to play with them. Lick them for me baby", I typed to Chayne.

Euftis Emery

Chayne easily lifted her large, full breasts to her lips and took turns sucking her hard nipples.

"Loooook…at…those…*nipples*…", Pumpkin purred and then circled her lips twice with the tip of her tongue wishing that one of Chayne's nipples was in her mouth.

"They are as wide as a nickel. Are they soft Daddy?"

"Very soft", I replied as I continued to watch Chayne suck on her tits with my friends. "And very sensitive. She'll suck my dick all night long and cum the whole time as long as I play with her breasts while I do it."

"*I got to get a computer. I got to get a damn computer*", Don grunted loudly as he began to pace around the room.

Pumpkin and I looked at each other and laughed at busting Don's webcam cherry. "I'm gonna take Don to my room and suck his dick really good", Pumpkin said as she took her man by the arm. "Have fun with your friend. I'll be back after I put him to sleep."

Chuckling with Pumpkin's nasty directness, I continued to chat with Chayne as Pumpkin walked Don up the stairs to her bedroom so that she could suck him off. Chayne became heated licking on her nipples and stood up on her bed and pealed out of jeans.

Sensing that things were going to get taken up a notch I called Chayne on my cell. "Hello…", she answered the phone giggling.

I'm Shy…

"What are you doing", I asked slyly.

Chayne sat back down on the bed and the view of her wide panty-clad hips was replaced by her large breasts and mischievous grin on her face. "You know how sensitive my breasts are baby. Suckin' on 'em has got me wet. Real wet. I need to play with it a bit."

She leaned back against the headboard, slid out of her panties and spread her long legs to the camera. Her pubic mound was smooth as a baby's bottom free of any blemishes or bumps and Chayne slowly ran her middle finger from the bottom of her slit up to her clit.

"You like my monkey baby", Chayne asked with the same mischievous grin etched on her face.

"I sure do", I lied in reply. The truth was I found her head (which was ScreaminToeCurlin Str8 fire) much more satisfying and intriguing than her pussy so I wasn't particularly moved when she showed it to me.

Chayne slid the tip of her long middle finger from the bottom of her slit up to her clit and moaned unashamedly in pleasure.

"It's…so…wet…", she breathed as she slid her finger back down and embedded it between her legs to her knuckle. She pulled the finger out slowly and it shined with wetness.

Chayne tilted her head back, lifted her wet finger to her mouth and swallowed her finger as if she were a knife swallower at a carnival licking it clean.

I repressed the urge to make a disgusted face. Don't get me

Euftis Emery

wrong, I love to watch a chick lick up her own juices I just didn't enjoy watching Chayne licking up her own. I'm comfortable with licking up a woman juices….when they are clear or resembling male pre-ejaculate. But if it's thicker or murkier than that my face goes nowhere near the pussy because in my mind there is something off with the woman's PH or she has some kind of infection. Yes…yes…I know the thickness and clearness can vary based on the time of the month, etc. so, don't none of you women with murky or thick pussy juice bombard me emails 'cause you're defensive about your shit. But my personal prejudice is that if a woman's lubrication isn't clear… There is something wrong with your shit and there will be…no…oral sex. But I digress…on with the story.

So Chayne continued to finger and lick her fingers thinking that she was turning me on while increasingly turning me off. I patiently waited for her to get sleepy after popping off a few orgasms and then told her goodnight so she could go to sleep. Pumpkin still had not come back downstairs, so I shut down Yahoo and logged onto BlackPlanet.Com to peruse the new ass that had recently joined the website.

Hands-down, BlackPlanet.Com is the…*best*…website in the world to hook-up with a chick and get some ass. You heard me right…it's the…*best*…hook-up site. Fling.com? Uhh uhhhh! AdultFriendFinder.Com? Don't make me laugh. OnLineBootyCall.Com? Sorry. Nope. Naw I must disagree! No, my horny friends. Doesn't matter if you're male or female if you're lookin' for a hot online fuck get an account on BlackPlanet.Com.

But I digress yet again. On with the story. So, as I said, I perused BP to check out the new ass that had joined the site

I'm Shy…

that month. I scrolled through the 20+ new prospects in the Cincinnati area and after not seeing anyone attractive or interesting enough then changed my search to bring back all females that joined that month in the Dayton area.

Although Dayton is only thirty minutes away from Cincinnati, the mindset and style of the women between the two cities is like night and day. With the women in Cincinnati being boring, closed-minded, and lacking in style and the women in Dayton being exciting, worldly and the dépêche mode in style.

Sure enough, the sixth profile down had exactly what I what I wanted. I opened the profile of my interest and beheld an extremely attractive high-yella, damn near white cutie in her thirties.   She had the thickness, with nice wide hips, big legs, succulent breasts, and a pretty face adorned by her long, blonde curly hair. I was very intrigued because she was dressed up like a stripper with heals on that had to be at least seven inches long. Here pictures screamed…*freak*. But what intrigued me more was her Personal Message which was concise and articulate.

Hello gentleman. My name is Aquino. I'm enjoying my time spent here on BP, however, don't be misled by the pictures that are on my page. Although I am very much a freak, there is much more to me than meets the eye (wink).

Please do not approach me from a strictly sexual perspective because I will ignore you. However, if you're a well spoken, intelligent, professional brother (that can handle his business…wink) then by all means send an email or IM to the address below.

Euftis Emery

I'm Shy…

I prefer professional men who know how to show a woman a good time. So, if you're not professional please do not attempt to contact me.

"How nice", I thought. "An articulate, educated…freeeeeak….Momma. Why I do believe I want to hit that."

I bounced back over to Yahoo and sent Aquino an email message and added her to my Yahoo messenger. She wasn't online, as I'd hoped, so I flipped back over to BP to continue salivating at her pictures and fantasize on how I'd fuck her. During my ogling of Aquino's pictures Pumpkin came back downstairs to check on me.

A smile appeared on my face as my best friend strolled regally down the steps. Pumpkin was such a classy temptress. She wore a dark green, vintage evening gown made from velvet with matching fur-lined mules. Her fitted evening dress flowed down to her shoes and was parted by a split in the front that ran all the way to her crotch and the v-neck at the top plunged down into the depths of her ample bosom.

As she strolled down the steps, she looked like Mae West from "*Gone With the Wind*" and I marveled at my best friends femininity. She casually walked over to the dining room table where I was sitting while she absent-mindedly pulled on the bottom of the pearl necklace that looped about her neck in three tight coils.

"I like your outfit", I told Pumpkin as I reached out and ran my hand along one of her sleeved arms so that I could feel the material. "Velvet. Very nice", I said as I ran my hand slowly up and down her arm. "You dressed up like this just

Euftis Emery

to suck Don off? You need to write a book Pumpkin. You know how to take care of a man."

"Bitches don't dress up for you Daddy", Pumpkin exclaimed surprised as she pulled on the bottom of her pearl necklace tightening the coils around her neck.

"Some women do. If we plan to get down in advance, then some women will dress up. But on a casual tip during the week… And just to give me head. I've…never…had a woman to do that for me."

"I don't know what's wrong with these modern-day bitches", Pumpkin began to preach pulling on the bottom of her pearls again tightening the coils around her neck unconsciously.

"My Mom raised me to take care of my man. You should cook for him, clean for him and suck a mean dick for him. Your man should never go so sleep and see you jacked up. Your hair needs to be done. Make-up on, nails done, toes done. His vision of you as he goes to sleep should be of you at your best. After...he goes to sleep is when you take the makeup off and put a scarf around your head. It took me all of five minutes to throw this on, but Don will remember this for a lifetime. If he were to ever leave me and get some modern day bitch every time he got with her in the back of his mind he would be comparing her shit with the little things like this that I did for him and he would be missin' me."

"Preach Pumpkin. Yes, he would be missing you. You need to write that book", I said seriously.

Pumpkin laughed and pulled on her pearls once again constricting her neck.

Euftis Emery

I'm Shy…

"I just found out something else about you Pumpkin", I said cautiously squinting my eyes.

"And what's that", Pumpkin replied confused.

"You like to be choked…

Pumpkin's eyes got wide as she realized what she had been unconsciously doing. "Awww...damn... Busted", she exclaimed giggling.

"You never told me that you liked to be choked Pumpkin", I replied a bit hurt.

"Only when I'm sucking dick", Pumpkin replied matter of fact.

Shocked by her response, my eyes grew wide.

"What did I say", Pumpkin asked nervously.

"Only that you like to be choked when you suck dick. Now if you said you liked to be choked...in general...I could get with that and I wouldn't have been shocked. But you had to fuck all that up and let me know that you got a...*specialized*...way that you like to be choked. Damn Pumpkin and I thought I was a freak!"

"Damn", Pumpkin replied giggling nervously. "I guess I told on myself again.

"So, what is it about being choked that you like baby? You remember Lucy? She likes that shit. But I just can't bring

I'm Shy...

myself to do it. I'd be scared that I'd hurt her."

"Well since the cat is out the damn bag I may as well tell you", Pumpkin replied smiling. "The whole process of sucking a man's dick is a submissive act all in of itself. Even more so when get on your knees or let a man fuck your hair all up while he's grabbing your head making you gag all over his shit. That shit turns me on", Pumpkin said with vehemence. "All my life my Mom, Grand Ma, and women at the church have drummed in my head that oral sex is something that a woman should never do. So even though I really wanted to...growing up...I never sucked dick. I didn't suck a dick until I was twenty-four and the nigga that I sucked had to mouth rape my ass. We was fucking around one night and he whipped that shit out and told me to suck it for him. I said...no. What the fuck I say that for? That nigga snatched me off the couch by my weave, threw me in a corner and stuck his big dick all down my throat Daddy. He called me every kind of bitch he could think of, pulled half my weave out, had tears streaming down my eyes, drooling all down my cleavage and every time I tried to resist he choked the shit out of me with the scarf I had on that night to make me act right. That...shit...turned...me...on Daddy!"

I simply stared at my friend wide eyed with an open mouth. Pumpkin always fucked me up with the things she was into.

"That nigga had a bitch so heated my pussy was...*gushing*...Daddy. I...begged...that mouth raping nigga to fuck me and he stood me up, raw dogged me in the corner really good and then mouth raped me some more making me lick all my juices off his dick and balls. I loved that shit! And since he...*took*...it I didn't have a bunch of guilt from all the things that have been drummed into me about oral sex.

Euftis Emery

I'm Shy...

That's why now when I plan on sucking some dick I'll put on some pearls or a scarf and tell a nigga to rough me up and choke me a bit 'cause even though I like it...I still hear my Mom's voice in my head every time I do it", Pumpkin said earnestly.

I just shook my head, which made Pumpkin laugh at me loudly looking at the expression on my face.

"*Don't...trip...Daddy*! You know you as just as big a freak as me, your ass just gets down in other ways. Speaking of which. What you looking at", Pumpkin asked as she peered at my monitor to see what I was doing.

"I'm trolling on BP checkin' out the new ass that joined this month. Check out this chick right here...", I said turning the monitor towards Pumpkin.   "She's gonna be my new friend."

Pumpkin's eyes grew wide as she gazed at my prey's main profile picture. It was a picture of her on all fours in the middle of her bed wearing nothing more than a black wife beater with a matching black thong and seven-inch stripper shoes.

"Ohhhhhh...my... She's...a...", Pumpkin began as she clutched her pearls.

"She's what baby...", I asked curious.

Euftis Emery

I'm Shy…

"She's a...ho...", Pumpkin replied meekly.

"Alright Ms.ThrowMeInACornerAnForceMeToSuckADick. How you gonna call my future friend a ho", I asked indigent.

"I'm just saying Daddy. Look at her! She's putting it all out there on her BP page. I mean I can be a nasty ho... But that's behind closed doors... For my man."

"Whatever Pumpkin. I just think she's a well-balanced freak."

Pumpkin laughed. "Well-balanced freak..."

"Yes. You just lookin' at her on all fours. Check her out from my eyes."

"From your eyes", Pumpkin exclaimed. "I'm looking at the same damn picture you are."

"No, you're not", I replied. Look at the...background...of her pic. She has a nice, neat and clean bedroom. That denotes she's domestic as well as sexy. Ain't nothing like a woman who can cook, clean...and...suck ya dick."

Pumpkin laughed.

"Look at her bed. That looks like brass and the comforter is leather. That denotes she's accustomed to having nice shit. She got her hair done. Toes and nails done, and her profile says she got kids. All that denotes she keeps it sexy...while...holding her shit down. Which you got to admit most women...don't...do. Babygurl got class and must be professional. Roll all that together...that's a top-notch bitch in my book. She's probably *putting it out there* as you said because although she wants a professional brother, she wants one who can put some serious thug lovin' on her ass. She loves to get her fuck on and is signaling that if you fuck with her you better be able to hang."

Pumpkin looked at the picture again from my perspective and her eyes grew wide in comprehension. "Damn! You got all that from one picture… And you're probably right. Alright Daddy… I apologize. I'll stop hating on your future friend."

"Thank you. Think about all the chicks on here who has a pic up with them in a jacked-up bathroom. Or in their bedroom with a hamper of dirty clothes in the background. Dead giveaway that she don't have her shit together. A chick like that…may…be good enough for a fuck. But if she is too nasty, she wouldn't even be good for that because you know her hygiene would be seriously suspect."

Pumpkin laughed. "Yea I remember a bitch that got ran off BP 'cause she took a pic of herself in the bathroom and she had a turd in the damn toilet. She didn't even notice and posted that shit on her page."

"Exactly", I replied as Pumpkin continued to laugh. "People will notice the obvious like the turd in that pic but not pay enough attention to notice in the background how messy or dirty someone's space. I…notice. If her space would have been jacked up, I wouldn't have stopped on her page."

"Well let me know how things go after you hit her up."

"You know I'm gonna give you full details baby", I replied.

"Okay…drool over your future friend later…I got a question",

I'm Shy…

Pumpkin whispered conspiratorially.

"Why you are whispering", I asked Pumpkin smiling.

"'Cause it's about Don", Pumpkin whispered.

"Well what's up", I asked.

"Have you ever heard of snowballing", she asked meekly.

I threw up a little bit in my mouth. The acid from my stomach burned my throat as I fought to swallow it back down and then had a coughing fit once I did.

"Are you alright", Pumpkin asked concerned.

I glared at Pumpkin as I took a big swig of my beer to get the taste of bile out of my mouth. "*Snowballing*", I exclaimed loudly as Pumpkin tried to hush me concerned.

Let me digress for bit. Snowballing is the human sexual practice in which one partner takes into their mouth the semen of another person, and then 'swaps' or passes it to the mouth of another, usually through kissing.

The term derives from the increased amount of liquid content produced as the semen, and accompanying saliva, is transferred from one mouth to another, "snowballing" into a larger amount as the act goes on.

Get it? If you didn't fully understand the definition straight from the dictionary, let me break it down for you. You...(woman or gay man) suck a dick until it cums in your mouth. Instead of swallowing it, you give your man a kiss and

Euftis Emery

pass the cum back into his mouth. The 'snowball' gets larger as it is passed because saliva is added to it. The passing continues until the snowball is so large that it can no longer be passed upon which the loser has to swallow it. *That's some nasty shit!* But I digress. On with the story.

"Not so loud", Pumpkin pleaded. "I don't want Don to hear what we are talking about. So, you know what it is?"

"Yea...", I replied disgusted in the same loud voice. "*That's some nasty shit*!"

Pumpkin blushed embarrassed. "What should I do? Don is my man and he has been asking me about this for a minute. Shouldn't I try to meet his needs?"

The irritation drained from my face upon seeing that my friend had a serious dilemma that she needed help dealing with. For a brief moment I was jealous that I hadn't found a woman like Pumpkin who loved me so much that she would do anything to please me...even if it pushed her out of her comfort zone. I didn't think Don deserved her but I suppressed my feelings, leaned back in my chair and tapped my foot for several minutes before answering. "Don got into that nasty shit fuckin' wit dem white gurls while he was over der in Europe in da military didn't, he?

Pumpkin giggled at my attempt to lighten the mood. "I don't know when he got into it but he's into it. Do you think I should try to meet his needs?"

"You're a good woman to want to try to meet your mans needs. But the operative word is your...man. He's not your husband. I personally don't think that you need to do something that pushes you out of your comfort zone for someone who is not your spouse.   However, a person should attempt to meet every need of their spouse. If your spouse wants something that you don't or can't do then you need to allow them to occasionally get what they need outside the relationship. So, my question for you is do you see spouse potential in Don?"

"Yes, I do Daddy", Pumpkin replied seriously. "I know that I complain allot to you about him, but we love each other, and we talk about our future together."

"Well if he is the one then you should try to meet his need. But is that something really that...you...want to do?"

"You know if It was up to me, I'd never bring it up", Pumpkin replied nervously.

"Then tell Don that he is free to get that nasty shit from someone else. If he's adamant that you participate, tell him you'll watch but you're unable to do that for him."

"Okay Daddy...", Pumpkin replied pensively.

"In a perfect world a person could find someone to meet all of their needs and vice versa. This ain't a perfect world baby. You're not gonna tell Don that he can't do it period. You're just gonna tell him he can't with you. But you're gonna give him the license to get it elsewhere. If I were in his shoes, I wouldn't have a problem with it, and he shouldn't either."

"Thank you, Daddy...", Pumpkin replied with more confidence. "I was really concerned that I was going to have to get into some shit I really didn't want to."

Euftis Emery

I'm Shy...

"Did you ask Don how he found out that he liked that nasty shit", I asked Pumpkin curious.

She shook her head signaling no and laughed.

"Well you should", I continued. "I always wonder how people get into nasty shit like that. I mean how does someone get into shit like snowballing, pissing on people, being shit on. Do they just sit up at night and think, "Damn. I think I want somebody to piss on me. I think that shit would turn me on."

Pumpkin hollered. "Maybe somebody accidentally pissed on them and they liked it."

"How can you accidentally piss on somebody", I asked flabbergasted as I continued to joke around with my best friend.

****

The following Monday I wasted no time and logged into Yahoo Messenger after work so that I could see if my new potential friend was online. I was excited to see that she was, and I fired off a short instant message in my *nice guy* persona. "Hi, I'm Euftis. Saw your profile on BP and I'm intrigued. How are you doing tonight?"

I waited five minutes to see if she would reply and when she didn't I left my computer and went downstairs to my office to watch television. Just because I sent her an instant message, I didn't expect her to...reply...instantly. It would piss me off whenever someone I didn't know who tried to get my attention on messenger got their panties in a bunch because I

I'm Shy...

failed to reply instantly. Just because I was online didn't necessarily mean I was also at the computer. People who made such an assumption with me were immediately dismissed and I had no intentions of doing the same with my new potential friend.

After watching three hours of television I went upstairs to my bedroom to go to bed but first checked my computer to see if Aquino had replied to my message. She hadn't and she was still online. Not making the assumption that she had seen my message I left my computer on and went to bed.

The next morning after getting up and getting ready for work, I checked my computer again to see that Aquino had logged off sometime that night after I went to bed and had failed to reply to my message.

There could only be two reasons why she failed to respond, and I briefly pondered it.   Either she was flat out rude which would downgrade her ranking. Or she was not interested in the *nice guy* approach and I would have to come much harder. Smiling to myself liking the challenge I shut down my computer and went to work.

Work was uneventful, and after getting home, doing a few chores, and fixing myself a bite to eat, I got back online to see if my friend was available. Like clockwork she logged on around 8pm and upon confirming her routine I opened up the document of my latest novel Keisha and I went to work putting in a few hours on my next book.

I deliberately didn't send her a message when I saw her log on to allow her time to get rid of the hounds and bug a boos who lurk about cyberspace waiting to pounce as soon as the

Euftis Emery

yellow smiley face of any female on their buddy list lit up.

All the women reading this who chat on the Internet know what I am talking about. It's easy to tell the difference between women who chat/hookup often on the internet from those who don't. Seasoned Internet freaks log on in...*invisible*...mode to avoid being hounded. While women oblivious to the extremes of sexuality on the Internet or just recently exposed to it naively revealed themselves to sex starved men hidden behind chat windows.

Since my prey's status was visible it was obvious that she was new to the game. But I knew that within a month she would tire of checking and cussing out men that she was not interested in hounding her and that she would begin to log on in invisible mode.

So, I waited patiently, giving her time to blow off everyone that she wasn't interested in before I pounced. After working for two hours I sent Aquino another instant message. "Good evening I'm Euftis. Checked you out on BP and I like what you have to offer. I fully meet your qualifications and I'd like to get to know you. Check out my profile (GetDeepInYou) on BP and let me know what's up."

Not bothering to wait for a reply I reopened my novel, Keisha, and began to put in some quality time on it. I had been working for little over an hour when a chat window popped up from my friend Mon Petite.

Not satisfied with just chatting with her, I sent her an invitation to view my webcam. She accepted the invitation and my computer began to stream video into her home, but she didn't return the favor as I had hoped.

I'm Shy…

Frowning I called Mon Petite on the phone.
"Hiiiiiiiiiiiieeeeeeee", she answered in her high-pitched voice
running together a salutation and my nickname.

"Bonjour Mon Petite. Hi yourself", I fired back frowning at
my camera knowing that was what she was seeing my
irritation on her computer.

"Bonjoooooour. Bonjour E. Commo alley vous?"

"Mad at you", I replied frowning harder.

"Qu'ai-je fait", she replied with humor in her voice.

"Speak in English Mon Petite", I barked. "I don't know that
much French."

"What did I do", she replied laughing.

"I got my cam on. Why ain't yours on", I replied acting every
bit of the spoiled brat that I was.

"I'm ready for bed. All I got on is a wife beater with no
makeup on."

"And...", I boomed. "Seen you both naked and with no
makeup on and I like both. Especially you naked. Turn your
cam on....damn it", I demanded.

"O...kay...damn it", she replied laughing mocking me.

Several minutes later I received a cam request and Mon
Petites cute features came into view. Her camera was angled

above her so that I could see her from the waist up and as she stated the only thing that she wore was a white wife beater.

Mon Petite had large, perpetually hard, oversized nipples on her shapely breasts, and they jutted out impressively against her white cotton tee shirt staining it with her dark flesh. I unconsciously licked my lips as I stared at them. I loved sucking, licking and touching them and wished I could treat myself to a snack that very second.

"You happy now", Mon Petite joked as she leaned forward on her desk and the angle of her camera provided a view that slid down her back allowing me to see a portion of her tramp stamp above the curvature of her ample buttocks.

"Just as round as two, big, ripe cantaloupes", I mumbled as I stared at Mon Petites impressive waist to ass ratio.

"What did you say", she asked playfully.

"I…said…your ass is as round as two, big ripe cantaloupes", I replied. "Lil fione ass! And the answer is…yes…I'm happy. Real damn happy!"

Mon Petite giggled which caused her dark brown eyes to twinkle and a sensuous smile to form on her beautiful lips. "Damn…", I breathed.

"What now", Mon Petite exclaimed.

"Those lips…", I replied. "Just about every part of you I wanna lick and suck on."

"Mmmmmm…thaaaank you…", Mon Petite purred blushing.

I'm Shy...

"Yooooou...tryin' to get back in my paaaanties."

"Technically I'm tryin' to get between your legs because you don't have any panties on!"

Mon Petite giggled again squeezing her thighs together.

"Speakin' about them lips I got something for ya", I continued as I moved Mon Petite's video feed to the left side of my monitor and drilled down into one of my photo folders with my mouse searching for a particular picture.

"What ya...got...for me", Mon Petite chirped as she bounced one time in her seat.

"Hold on a second", I replied as I looked around in another folder. Upon finding the picture I wanted, I dropped it into the chat window to send it to my friend.

"What's this...", Mon Petite asked a little excited bringing another smile to my face. Her cute personality was infectious.

The file downloaded quickly, and Mon Petite opened it.

Euftis Emery

I'm Shy…

"Ohhhhhhh…my lips! How did you do this? What you gonna do with 'em", she asked curious and flattered.

"I scanned them from the lip prints that you put on my birthday card", I replied. I'm going to print and frame them."

"Frame them for what", Mon Petite asked confused.

"For my wall. I'm going to blow the picture up…print it on glossy photo paper…and put them on my wall", I replied elaborating. "You've got some sexy ass lips. They'll make a nice contemporary art piece."

Mon Petite's eyes went wide for several seconds. And then she looked down composing herself but blushed uncontrollably, nonetheless. She was a nuclear bomb of emotion and passion but always fought to keep them contained and hidden. I knew that I had moved her deeply even though she pretended that I didn't.

"Yoooooou…tryin' to get back in my paaaaanties", she joked again.

"No sweetie…I…*will*…be in your panties again. Don't play", I replied.

Mon Petite didn't comment not wanting to display one ounce of her feelings. "I need your help E", she said changing the topic.

"Need my help with what?"

I'm Shy…

"A friend of mine is trying to get his girlfriend into doing threesomes with him. He asked me if I would talk to you about giving him some pointers."

"Why does he think that I can help him", I asked.

"He's In your Yahoo group and he's seen the advice that you've given in your "Who's your Daddy" advice column."

"Another one of those Negroes who join my group and never say anything", I growled.

I had a Yahoo Group with several thousand members made up of 80% females and 20% males. The males never participated, purchased any of my books and hated on me clandestinely making negative comments about me and my work behind my back. So, I was not the least bit interested in doing a favor for a faceless person who never did anything for me.

"NoPussyGettinNegro wants me to share my player wisdom and he never even made one comment in my group", I began as I started to go off. "And I'm sure he never got one of my books. His NoPussyGettinAss can go to hell. I ain't doin…"

"E…", Mon Petite interrupted my tirade in a soft voice. "Do it for me."

"Ummmm…okay", I replied simply. "I'll talk to him."

Mon Petite is one of the few people that can ask anything of me, and she knows it. However, although she knows it, she would never abuse the privilege.

Euftis Emery

I'm Shy...

"He's online right now. Can I conference him in?"

"Sure...go ahead sweetie", I replied.

Mon Petite stood up and her small waist, hips and shaved pubic mound filled the camera filled the camera for several seconds. She came back into view several minutes wearing a thick, white robe.

"Heeeeeey....why'd you put that on", I protested.

"Because I'm going to bring him into our cam chat. I don't know him like that!"

Mon Petite sent a cam request to her friend and once he accepted his camera began to feed to my workstation.

"E this is Mike. Mike...E", Mon Petite said happily making introductions.

"What's up", I asked Mike quickly getting to the point.

"Thanks for talking to me Euftis", the young brother replied. "I've been a member of your group for a couple of months now and I'm really enjoying it."

"Whatever", I thought. "You've never said a word, probably don't have one of my fuckin' books and would be cock blockin' with Mon Petite if you knew I was hittin' it!"

"I have a question for you... How can I get my gurl to do a threesome with another sexy young lady? Any suggestions, advice or...regrets", he asked snickering.

I'm Shy…

"Has your girl told you or have you noticed that she's into girls? If she does like girls, does she prefer girls or is she more partial to dick? If your girl told you that…yes…she'll do a threesome with you if you return the favor and let her bring a certain big dick brother home to fuck and lick her senseless while you watched would that bother you? Have you ever asked your girl to tell you about her sexual experiences that she had with other men and/or women and did it turn you on to the point where you masturbated", I asked in rapid-fire succession.

Mike became tight lipped and wide-eyed. "If you're to uncomfortable to answer these questions, don't bother. You're not ready to have a threesome with your girl", I said seriously.

"My girl has noticed women and made some comments but nothing to heavy. I have some idea that she used to be into women somewhat just through casual conversation. She has brought it up a few times but when I tried to dive deeper into what she's done she clams up. I know for a fact that a few of her friends are bi and some are outright lesbians. And these ladies have been her friend's way before I was around. I believe she is partial to dick and if she did agree to have a threesome with me and wanted me to return the favor I would. I am secure in who I am that even if they guy was King Kong, I wouldn't have a problem with it. My girl told me on several occasions about her past sexual experiences and none of it made me uncomfortable", Mike confessed.

Since Mike answered my questions satisfactorily, I decided to drop knowledge on him to help him turn out his girl.
"Alright go get a pen and some paper so you can take notes", I stated blandly.

Euftis Emery

I'm Shy...

Mon Petite giggled.

"Take notes...", Mike stammered.

"Yes... Take notes. Pimpin'...ain't easy... I'm here to tell ya.
Do you really want to do this or what?"

Mike looked a little unsure and then got up to get a pen and
some paper. He sat back down in front of his camera five
minutes later. "Alright... Got my pen and paper", he replied a
little sarcastically.

Alright. Be sure to take good notes because I will not be
repeating this", I replied not liking his attitude.

"If your girl already has an attraction to females then the first
thing that you need to do is get her to...admit...that she digs
girls. You need to get her comfortable with the concept of a
threesome and she can't get there if she can't first admit to
herself that she likes pussy other than her own."

"You need to use a...subtle...approach and manipulate her on
a subliminal level", Mike's eye grew wide.

"Yes, I said manipulate...don't trip. It's all fair in love and
war. What you need to do Mike is expose her to women that
she finds attractive so that she will become aroused and begin
to fantasize about females and you can also get a feel for the
type of women that she likes."

"The key here is initially do not...mention...what you are up to
or comment when she comments or looks at other women.
Just note what she likes."

Euftis Emery

I'm Shy...

"Some of the things you can expose her to is a church with a large congregation, the hot spot in town where everyone goes, a swingers club, strip club etc. Expose her to places and events where there is a large number of attractive, well dressed, or scantily dressed women. In these types of venues not only will she see women...but women who are bi or gay will pick up her vibe, approach her and engage her in conversation. Got it", I asked Mike giving him the opportunity to catch up as he scribbled furiously.

"This is good... This is good...", Mike replied excited. "Got it!"

"Your girl sounds like one of those *HolierThanThou* females. She's quick to look down on something and let you know it. But every now and then she'll begin to tell you about some stank shit in her past and get silent when you ask too many questions. FYI, dawg...it's been my experience that females like that tend to be scandalous beyond belief. I'd turn around quick to see what she was doing every time I turned my back if I were you. I turn women like that out. But I'd never make one my woman. That's just my two cents", I said seriously as Mike appeared to get a little angry with my side comment but didn't say anything.

"Moving on", I continued after giving my comment several seconds to sink in. "I propose you use this approach with your girl... Take her regularly to the large happen' church in town that has a lot of single members and start having a...movie...night with her."

"Take her to church", Mike exclaimed laughing.

Euftis Emery

I'm Shy...

"Yes! Take her ass to church", I replied forcefully. "You will not believe how many bisexual and lesbian women are up in the church every Sunday. I don't think you will be able to get your girl into a strip or swingers club, but if you propose to take her to church, she will be blind-sided. Set her ass up dawg!"

Mike laughed loudly as he continued to take his notes.

"Within couple of visits there will be gay women pushin' up on her trying to be her friend. Let that shit happen and don't comment. Just watch her eyes at all times to gauge what she likes."

"Two, start having a movie night with her. Pick a day in the week and propose that the two of you have some...quiet time...together to just chill. Make sure the movie you pick every week has lesbian content."

"Here is an example of how I used the movie night to turn out one particular female. The first night I brought the movie "Show Girls" over to her house. We watched the movie until I noticed that she was getting uncomfortable because she was getting turned on and then I jumped her ass."

"The next week I followed up with "Bound". The week after that I hit her with the "Player's Club". Every week I jumped her as...soon...I noticed that she was uncomfortable or aroused."

"After we watched "Player's Club" I knew what she liked. Thick, big booty having sisters. So, the next week I brought a porno of Vanessa Blue and Kat fucking each other. Her

34

pussy was never wetter."

"While I hit it, I made her admit she liked girls. You liked watchin' them big booty girls lickin' each other...didn't you! Didn't you!"

"Yes! Yes", she screamed while I hit it.   "Awww...it was on after that ...believe it!"

"Now...after she admits she likes girls...then...you broach the subject of a threesome. I'll let you digest this for a minute and then I'll break down how you set the threesome up. I'll be right back going to get something to drink", I told Mike as I got up from my computer.

I had taken two steps when my phone rang. Turning around to retrieve it from my desk as it vibrated my phone let me know who was calling by displaying the image of Mon Petite in a skintight, short pink dress.

"What's up sexy", I said as I bounced down the steps headed downstairs to get a drink.

"You know I'm sitting over here in awe...right", she said. "I knew you were gonna break it down but...*damn*", she remarked giggling.

"What...", I asked innocently as I poured a glass of cranberry juice.

"You...are...a...manipulative...ass", Mon Petite stated shocked. "Oooooohhhhh...my God!"

"It's all good sexy", I replied as I headed back up the steps to my bedroom. "Women manipulate men and men manipulate women. It's the natural order of things in the continuing war between the sexes."

"But you're so...*premeditated*...with your shit. Oooooooooohhhh...my God!"

"Whateva...", I replied feigning to be upset as I sat back down at my desk and glared at Mon Petite through my camera.

"We'll pick this up later", Mon Petite said giggling. "Continue. This is a damn education."

I sighed pretending to be exasperated. "Moving on", I continued.

"Setting up the threesome. After she admits to herself vocally that she digs girls, continue to expose her to bi-girl shit. Now you can begin commenting when you catch her looking or commenting about other women. Don't get upset if initially she's closed lipped if you catch her looking at another woman and you ask what she likes/wants to do to her, and she doesn't say anything. Just keep commenting every time you catch her. By commenting you are doing two things."

"One. Putting shit firmly in her head. By prompting her...'you like that don't you? What would you do to her? Although she may not...say...anything to you she will think about what you asked her."

"Two. Slowly but surly she will see that you really don't have a problem with her checking out other girls."

I'm Shy…

"As she gets more comfortable answering your questions when you catch her watching/commenting on other chicks then…you…begin to comment on women that you think are attractive and tell her point blank what you would do to her if you got your hands on her."

"She needs to get comfortable with the concept of the two of you fucking the same woman and talking about it will get the two of you there."

"While you are working her, share pictures and tell bi-sexual or gay women who are good friends of yours and who have a history of turning out straight women about your woman and her curiosity of fucking girls. It's important they are…good…friends you can trust. I'll get into why later. If you don't have any…make…some or talk to close friends of yours who have some close gay friends."

"If you have nude photos of your girl share 1-3 of them with your gay friends and ask them for details of what they would do to your girl. Write the details down if you can't remember. It's critical that you remember the details of what they say even if its mundane details like…I'd like to see your girl in a coral bra and panty set when I fuck her…"

"Your girl needs to…hear…how another woman see's her so remember the details of what the gay women tell you. Don't leave out a detail because you think it's boring or stupid. She's doing a…girl. Not a man. They get down differently. By the way, make sure the gay friend lives in a different town than you."

"You still with me", I asked concerned because Mike wasn't asking any questions.

Euftis Emery

I'm Shy...

"I'm getting all this down. You're good", Mike replied smiling.

"Cool. Now, once your girl is comfortable, and talks to you about other women when either you or her mentions them and you have a gay friend in your pocket whose dying to fuck your girlfriend...now...you are ready to drop the bomb on her."

"How do you do it", I continued not giving Mike the chance to ask. "Casually. Say over breakfast, lunch, or coffee. Chat with her merrily and then say something like... Hey! By the way. I've got a friend. And she...*loves*....to eat pussy. I showed her a couple of pictures of you...and she said she would looooove to eat the fuck out of you."

Mike laughed.

"Say it nonchalantly. You know like you're discussing the weather. And while your girl stares at you...blushing if she's light enough you continue. So, you know I told my friend I'm cool with it. So...whenever...you want your pussy licked. You just let...me...know. My friend is just...*dying*...*to* eat you.

Mike laughed again.

"Now your girlfriend is going to act a little upset that you shared some naked pics of her without telling her...but you just ignore her ire and tell her in detail what your gay friend said about her pics and what she would do to her. Pull out your notes if you need them."

"You're girlfriend will play like she's mad but she'll really be flattered and intrigued and ask you what your gay friend looks like and if you have done you're home work you picked a women she will like…and you will just happen to have some nude pics of your gay friend in your pocket so you can whip them right out and show her."

"Now, as your girl stares at the pics and imagines what it will be like to get her pussy ate out by another woman she's going to ask you a question…", I said hesitating giving Mike an opportunity to figure out the answer.

"I don't know. What will she ask me", Mike asked confused?

"The question that she will ask is…what will she want me to do to her? And your reply will be…", I said hesitating again.

Mike look woefully confused so I continued his education patiently. "You will tell her that she won't have to do…anything. That your friend will just want to…eat her."

Mike smiled in realization seeing the subtly of my insidious trap.

"That's right… When you jump this off, you will ensure that your gay friend only eats your girl out. For two reasons:"

"One. You want your girl to be turned the fuck out so that she looks forward to getting with other women. you don't want her to balk at the act by telling her that she has to do shit. She will be nervous enough as it is and more so since she doesn't know what she is doing. She will be more inclined to go along with things if all she has to do is lay back and enjoy getting served."

I'm Shy...

"Two. By letting her know that you will only watch she will not have the added anxiety of wondering how she will act seeing you with another woman."

Mike frowned upon hearing my second point.

"Awwwww...and you thought it was all about you? Didn't you? Don't fret. Once she's turned out you will get yours and then some."

"Now, she's going to have another question for you."

I continued not wasting further time asking him to guess. "When is this going to happen?"

"You're reply?"

"Ohhhhh....I don't know. I'm just letting you know...you know...what my friend said. So, when...you...want it to happen...you just let me know."

"Now...if your girl proposes a date by all means...hook that shit up! But if she doesn't...then you want to throw her into the water. Literally! So, don't give her any warning when it's going to happen. Let two to three weeks go by without mentioning a thing and plan an event that your gay friend attends and let her sleep over."

"After you plan the event (i.e., party, concert etc) and your girl agrees to go...then...you mention casually...ohhhh by the way....you know that friend i told you about....you know...the one who wants to eat your pussy? Well she's coming down and asked if she could spend the night. I told her it was okay."

I'm Shy...

"Now your girl will be in shock. But reassure her that's its cool. And when your gay friend gets there just have her...*take your girls shit!"*

"Just like that", Mike asked.

"Just...like...that", I replied. "Okay. Now you had your first threesome. Albeit you only got to watch the first time. But now your girl's turned out and wants to learn more about the joys of girls. It's all good.   Right", I asked.

Mike shook his head smiling.

"Wrong", I fired back bringing a frown of confusion to Mike's face.

"Check it out", I continued. "Make sure you set up the threesome to last over a weekend. That way your gay friend can hit your girlfriend's shit a couple of times before she rolls out to ensure that she is good and turned out."

"Now, after your gay friend leaves your girlfriends head will be fucked up. She just fucked a girl over the weekend and loved it. I mean... Imagine how you would feel if you let a dude suck on your dick over a weekend! That shit would fuck with your head big time", I said in a straight face making a joke at Mike's expense and I chuckled a bit as his face went blank from not appreciating the joke.

"Moving on", I continued smiling. "So, don't trip on your girl if she appears withdrawn and really doesn't want to talk. It's going to take her some time to process what she has done. Don't try to cuddle with her or worse treat he like a

Euftis Emery

child by telling her...you're proud of her or some other shit like that."

"My advice is don't do that. What you should do is....nothing. Let her deal with her head on her own and do not comment on what happened and just go on like nothing happened."

"Do this for 2-3 days which should give your girlfriend ample time to process what she did. Then you drop the bomb. Ask this question... So, baby tell me. What do you think after having your first threesome?"

"Pay very close attention to what she says next", I told Mike seriously as I paused a bit making sure that he got every detail. "She is going to say one of four things after you ask your question.

"One...I am never going to do that again! It was nice experiencing, but I am not going to ever do that again!"

"Now if your girl let your gay friend eat her pussy several times over the weekend until her head almost exploded you...know...that she's fulla shit! This type of female is a scandalous undercover ho! Ohhh she's gonna do it again. Just not with...you!"

"This type of female will try to get with your gay friend on the DL to expand her studies while spouting monogamy to you. When your gay friend (and this is why she needs to be Close to you) gives you that call and tells you that your girlfriend tried to snake that pussy.

Your only recourse is to dump that ho on general principle! Cause if she will fuck a close friend of yours, she'll fuck...anyone...close to you with no remorse."

"Two... I really enjoyed that. I was scared at first. But when she started licking my pussy it was a wrap! I loved it. I can't wait to get with another girl again!"

"I bet you think you should dance a jig if she says something like that don't you? Nope! You are fucked! Congratulations... You just created a full-fledged lesbian. Notice the operative word in her statement was "I"! She didn't mention...shit...about you! If she says something like this, she doesn't know it yet...but she prefers pussy...over your dick."

"My advice to you if this happens is...walk away! The reason is that she's gonna swing with you. Whole heartedly. You are gonna have a good time...and get caught up! But your good time is going to come to a screeching halt when she figures out for herself, she loves pussy exclusively and leaves your ass for a woman."

"Listen to me now! If that happens don't go sending an email to the group talkin' bout..."...how do I get my gay girlfriend back... I ain't gonna wanna hear that shit! I'll talk about your ass!"

"The third thing she may say is I really enjoyed that baby. I want to experience more with you. When can we do something like that again?"

"Not that's what you want to hear! The operative words that you should hear are "you", "we", "us". If you hear any of those words in her response you have a woman who sees a threesome as an extension of her relationship with you.

I'm Shy...

That's what you want."

"Now, do you still want to have a threesome? There is a 60% chance that your relationship will end in the attempt. Take your time. Be patient."

"Damn you broke that shit down", Mike said amazed. "Thank you."

"You're welcome and good luck", I replied. "Let me know how it turns out."

Mike logged out of the chat leaving me looking at Mon Petite shaking her head. "You are a... swinger", she exclaimed.

"I did that for...you...baby. That nigga needs to pay me a monthly dividend for the knowledge I dropped on him today."

"Well I appreciate that E. Thaaaaaank...you", she replied seductively.

"Mmmmmm...you're...so very welcome lil sexy ass", I replied. *"I cannot wait to fuck you again"*, I thought.

Mon petite signed off and I scrolled through my buddy list to see if Aquino was still online. She wasn't and yet again she did not reply to my message. Two strikes. It was time to play hardball.

My Yahoo avatar was a nice carton caricature of me with a pet dragon at my side. It was cute and non-offensive. It really wasn't my style. I preferred using images far nastier but didn't because I never knew when a square friend or new fan would pop up on my IM and be offended from seeing an X-rated image.

However, now it was time to play hardball. I was going to come at Aquino str8 nasty with the freaky deke approach. If she didn't respond to that then it would be strike three and I would be out.

After a quick scroll through some past pictures I used for my Yahoo avatar I decided to go with a close shot of me hitting Tina's shit from the back. The picture spoke volumes on how I handled my business. Half the dick was buried deep in her pussy which overflowed punany juice. The part of the shaft that was submerged in pussy was lathered with creamy girl cum. Her left ass cheek was having the life squeezed out of it with one of my hands while the right ass cheek was blushed red from repeated smacks and her chocolate starfish was clenched tight as the picture caught her in the midst of yet another hard orgasm.

There wasn't any space between dick and pussy showing how my girth can fill it up. The picture left no doubt that a pussy got fucked...very...well on that day. Any true freak that looked at it would instantly know this and be curious what that dick would feel like within her.

Smiling after baiting my hook I logged out of Yahoo and went to bed. If Aquino was a true freak. She wouldn't be able to resist taking a bite of my bait.

As soon as I got home the next day after work, I electronically threw my virtual bait into cyberspace by logging into Yahoo Messenger. I knew my new avatar would be shining brightly on Aquino's monitor and went downstairs to

I'm Shy…

fix some dinner as I patiently waited for her to take the bait.

I grilled up some thin cut pork chops on the George Forman with some cabbage on the side and after eating that healthy meal I washed a load of clothes before venturing back up the steps to my bedroom.

After sitting down at my desk to do some writing, I glanced at my buddy list and confirmed that Aquino was online. I smiled knowingly as I sensed that I finally used the correct approach in capturing my prey.

Ten minutes had not passed before I finally received a message. "Heeeeey...is that you", Aquino asked.

I smiled. My prey took the bait and was hooked. Now I just needed to sit back and reel her in. "Excuse me", was my reply.

"Is that...you", she asked again.

"What? Is that my...*dick*...in that pussy", I replied.

"LOL", Aquino replied. "Mmmmmmmm....yes! Is that...your...dick in that pussy."

"Why yes, it is", I replied. "Why would I use someone else's dick?"

"Can I get some of that", Aquino replied bluntly.

I smiled. "*Hooked, netted and pulled in the boat*", I thought. "Ohhhh...look at you talkin' shit", I replied. "I don't know if you can. What you working with?"

Euftis Emery

I'm Shy...

"What do you mean", she asked.

"What you workin' with? Send me some pics of you...naked", I replied qualifying my prey.

I have very rigid qualifications when it comes to getting with a woman. First and foremost, she has to be a str8 freak. *A three-hole girl.* If you don't know...you better be ready to try. One who loves...not like...*loves*...to be fucked in...*every*...hole. Mouth, pussy and ass. On top of that she needs to be...*submissive.* When I tell her to hike that shit up in the air she doesn't hesitate or ask a fucking question...*just does it.*

When I pull out the handcuffs...*she's with it.* Doesn't matter if I tie her hands up behind her back, to the bed post or the damn chandelier. And when she's sucking the skin off my dick and I take her by the back of the head and tell her to drain it... She sucks me. *Dry!* Then licks her lips, looks me dead in the eyes and...*begs*...for Daddy to give her more. *I want to get my fuck on!* And if a bitch ain't with it...*I don't want it!* I don't give a fuck...*what*...you look like.

So, my first question was a test of home girls submissiveness and freakiness. A submissive woman follows the instructions of her Daddy without question. If she argued or outright refused my request, then she wouldn't be worth my time.

"Gimme a second", Aquino replied.

I waited patiently assuming that she was looking for a picture and it didn't take long for me to find out that my assumption was correct.

Euftis Emery

I'm Shy…

"Here's a couple of pics", Aquino typed over the IM as my computer prompted me to accept two images and sent me a request to see her webcam.

I downloaded the pictures, approved her webcam request, and opened the first picture. An image of my new friend filled my computer screen. It was a breast shot of my girl wearing a fur coat and no shirt or bra.

She cupped her full breasts into the camera and her dark pink nipples jutted impressively between her spread fingers.

Thus far she was passing with flying colors and I licked my lips wondering what it would feel like rolling my tongue on her raised flesh.

"Do you have a cam", Aquino asked with a playful expression on her face as her video fed cam into focus.

Unconsciously, I sent Aquino a web cam request and then opened the second picture.

"Ohhhhhhh...myyyyyyyyy...", I moaned making a fuck face. "I'dddddd...lick...that...."

"You'd lick what", Aquino asked with smiling light blue eyes.

"Snap! Busted...", I forgot that I sent Aquino a camera request. She could now see and hear me. "Ummmm...I just opened the pussy pick you sent me. I'd...lick...that... It's pretty."

I'm Shy…

"So that's why you're making that…face", Aquino exclaimed as she busted out laughing.

"Damn. Doubly busted", I replied as I ran a hand down my face smoothing it out.

"You're handsome", Aquino stated smiling.

"Thank you", I replied as checked out Aquino's surroundings. She was in her bedroom and it was as neat and tasteful as it appeared in her pictures. "What's your sign", I asked continuing my qualification process.

"I'm a Pisces."

"Yes…", I thought. "That's what I'm talkin' 'bout!"

The freak-alecks of the zodiac are the Cancers, Libra's, Sagittarius' and last but not least the Pisces. I have a list of qualifying questions for the other signs to determine if they are a three-hole freak but when girlfriend said she was a Pisces…I knew it was on!

"Really? I'm a Pisces. My birthday is on the 18th. When is yours", I replied?

"Really? My birthday is on the 17th", Aquino replied energetically.

"It'll be easy to remember your birthday. You've got a unique look. What are you mixed with?"

"I'm Polynesian and White", Aquino replied.

Euftis Emery

I'm Shy...

"*Interesting...*", I thought. "So, what's up? What you doing this Friday", I asked pushing to meet now that I had qualified my new friend.

"This Friday is my son's birthday so I'm gonna be spending time with him."

"What's up with Saturday then", I asked wanting to get up with girlfriend quickly while things were hot.

"Saturday is good for me...what you want to do?"

"I wanna get to know you so why don't we do the dinner and a movie thing. Let's do Cheesecake Factory at the Green then catch a flick."

Helpful hint number 5. Now there are some *NoPussyGettinNegros* reading this right now thinking that I should be pressing girlfriend for more pictures, trying to have webcam sex with her or telling her in detail what I'd do with her body parts. Wrong! Again, you only ask for pics or video to...qualify...that a chick is a freak. Once you've established that she is and that she's feeling you there...will...be fuckin'. So, there's no need to talk about it because you're going to be...doing it. So, don't talk shit or show them you don't get much pussy by pressing them for video or phone sex before you ever meet... You'll get the panties quicker.

"Okay. That sounds nice", Aquino replied. "What side of town are you on?"

"I live in Cincy", I replied. "What side of town are you on?"

"Ohhhhh...you live in Cincinnati", Aquino exclaimed. "I'm

Euftis Emery

I'm Shy...

on the south side of town. Near U.D."

I shook my head. "*Girlfriend probably never even read my profile*", I thought. "Cool, I'll pick you up then. What's your address?"

Aquino typed her address in the IM window, and I googled the directions to make sure that she wouldn't be too out of the way for me to pick her up. "Love your nails by the way", I said making conversation. They were painted in an intricate colorful design that was different from her pictures and I was quite pleased. Most men's attraction to women is influenced by their mother and I fit the norm. My mother was perpetually fly with the hair, nails, toes, and makeup flawless at all times. With my mother being the example of how a woman should be I sought the same in potential mates. Thus, Aquino's glamorous appearance seriously turned me on.

"Alright then. Let me get off here. I need to take care of a few things before I go to bed", I stated intentionally cutting the conversation short. Helpful hint number 37 fellas. First impressions are the best. So, after impressing a chick to the point that she gives up the digits or better yet confirms a date with you...*stop talking!* You don't want to have an awkward moment, say something stupid, or get in an argument over something petty and talk yourself out of getting some pussy. After you wax that ass well you can get away with saying something stupid every now and then. However, until you wax that ass keep the conversation light and trivial, plan a date and then...*shut the fuck up!*

"You logging off", Aquino asked surprised.

"Yea...it's a workday tomorrow... I go to bed early. Gimme

Euftis Emery

I'm Shy…

the digits before I log off. I'm sure we'll talk again before Saturday", I replied ending the conversation.

Aquino typed her number into the chat and after copying it I said goodnight and then logged off. Giddy with my success, I picked up my phone and called my partner in crime...Pumpkin.

"Hey Daddy, how you doin'", Pumpkin's pleasant voice rang out over the receiver.

"I...am...well baby", I replied in a merry voice. "Mission accomplished!"

"What do you mean", Pumpkin asked giggling.

"My...new...friend... It's on!"

"Ohhhhh...your blonde friend", Pumpkin asked.

"Yea... We goin' out on Saturday. I can't wait to hit it."

"You...are...too much", Pumpkin said laughing.

"What...", I asked confused.

"You just...*know*...you're gonna hit it on the first date", she replied amazed.

"Don't everybody get it on the first date", I asked still confused.

Pumpkin laughed again. "Daddy...I may be a freak...but even I will make a guy I'm dating wait for at least three months

Euftis Emery

I'm Shy...

before I let him hit it."

"GetTheFuckOuttaHere'", I exclaimed.

"I'm serious. Even if I'm lusting over a guy, I'll still make him
wait for at...least...a month. Every woman I know will make a
man wait a minute before they give it up... But you... Every
bitch you get with you in the drawers on the first date.
Damn", Pumpkin said amazed.

"Well I thought that's just how it goes down when two
people are feeling each other."

"Don't pay me no mind Daddy. I'm just always amazed with
your game. I'm sure you are gonna get it because you said so.
Let me know how the pussy is after you do."

"I will", I replied. "Check your mail."

"What you send me", Pumpkin asked puzzled.

"Girlfriend sent me some pics", I replied. "Check it out."

Pumpkin told me to hold on as she logged into her email so
that she could look at the pictures that I sent her.

"*Damn*", Pumpkin yelled excited.

"Like that do you", I asked smugly.

"Hell yea", Pumpkin replied. "Hook that shit up!"

I laughed. Pumpkin was always trying to fuck my girlfriends.
"The other day you were turning up your nose and calling my

Euftis Emery

I'm Shy…

friend a ho…now you want to hit it."

"Hook…that shit up", Pumpkin replied seriously.

I laughed again at my friend's lusty spirit. "I ain't hit it yet and you telling me to hook some shit up."

"I wanna…*fuck*…that…bitch", Pumpkin replied as I imagined her drooling over my friend's pictures. "So, after you hit it… Hook…that…shit…up…"

Her response caused me to laugh a third time. "I'll see what I can do…", I replied sarcastically.

****

Saturday finally came and I wavered on what I should wear for my date. It was late fall and I wanted to wear denim, but I was torn between Johnny Blaze, Pure Playaz or Pelle Pelle. Stumped on what would attract my prey the best I threw the jacket and matching pants to each outfit on my bed and yelled downstairs for the girls to come up and give me their opinion.

As usual, Sade made it to the room first followed by Elise then after calling for a second time my eldest, Nicole, finally made it to the room frowning as usual. I discussed my dilemma with the girls and then stepped back so they could give me their opinion.

All of them gave thumbs down on my front-runner, the carbon Johnny Blaze, not liking the huge, black skull and bones that took up most of the back of the jacket. They then deliberated amongst themselves between the Pure Playaz and

Euftis Emery

I'm Shy...

Pelle Pelle.

"What you gonna wear with them", Nicole asked not being able to make a decision.

Going to my closet, I pulled out a blue, patterned Perry Ellis dress shirt and some brown leather Giorgio Burtini dress shoes for the Pure Playaz and thick, black, long sleeved Pelle tee and black Kenny Cole boots to go with the Pelle Pelle.

"You gonna wear the shirt in or out", Nicole asked in regard to the Pure Playaz outfit.

"I'm gonna wear it out", I replied.

"Then wear that", Nicole replied, and her sisters co-signed emphatically.

"Thank you girls", I replied pleased. Being young women, I always asked for their opinion on what I planned on wearing on a date. I got the best reactions from my dates when I did.

After getting dressed I proceeded to Dayton, Ohio, which was a forty-five-minute drive from my home. As soon as I hit the city limits, I jumped onto I35 and proceeded to the west side of town.

Dayton is one of the few places where I watch my back at all times. It may not be a major metropolitan area, but size doesn't matter when jobs are scarce and folks are hungry for all of the finer things in life. I didn't fuck around in Dayton because Negroes there be wildin' out, but I was relieved the Aquino didn't live in the hood as I drove through the upper middle class west side.

Euftis Emery

I'm Shy...

After briefly getting lost, I eventually drove onto Aquino's dimly lit street and pulled up to her attractive two-story home. I was impressed. Her lawn was a healthy shade of green and immaculately trimmed. Her Denali truck was detailed and the 22's gleamed with Armor All. Aquino was holding it down and I couldn't wait to see what the inside of her house looked like.

I hit the steps in a single bound and then quickly rang her bell. She must have heard me pull up because before my hand could return to my side after ringing the bell the door quickly swung open and a smiling woman jumped into my space two feet in front of me.

I was taken aback. It was not Aquino. An extremely attractive, dark skinned woman with large dark brown eyes, jet black, silky hair and perfect white teeth stood before me grinning from ear to ear. She was a stark contrast to the damn near white, blonde and blue-eyed woman that I came to see, and I was caught totally off guard.

"*Choooooocolate...*", I thought liking what I saw and wanting a piece of it. But that's another story. :0)

"Hi Euftis. I'm Bridget. Aquino is getting ready. C'mon in", she said playfully turning giving me a close-up view of her ample backside. I discreetly licked my lips upon seeing her juicy bubble butt wanting to hit it. But I digress. Like I said...that's...another story.

I took my eyes off Bridget's ass after crossing the threshold and paused for a minute to take in my surroundings. The door opened into the living room and it was tastefully

Euftis Emery

I'm Shy...

decorated with contemporary furniture. A light brown, leather couch with two matching chairs on either end focused on a 50" Panasonic Hi-Def television.

I sat down in the extremely comfortable leather chair nearest the door after Bridget informed me that she was going to get Aquino. She walked to the end of the living room into the adjoining dining room and then proceeded into another room that was out of my line of vision. I assumed it was the kitchen and immediately realized that Aquino wasn't...getting ready...as Bridget had informed but that she had sent her friend to check me out and Bridget was now filing her...report...with her girl.

Looking into the dining room, I was further impressed with Aquino's decorating skills. She had decorated a black lacquer dining table with stylish green Asian tableware and Japanese prints adorned the walls throughout the house.

"*This is a woman that I could co-habitat with*", I thought loving the style and cleanness of her home.

I then turned my attention to Aquino's daughter and son who had not bothered to say a word to me or look up from the intense game of Madden football that they were playing. Their behavior let me know that they were used to strange men coming to see their mother and they were ambivalent about it. "*Playette...*", I thought.

As I continued to wait patiently for Aquino, her children finished playing each other and the boy began playing the computer while Aquino's mini-me fumbled with a new wireless headset as she attempted to sync it with her phone.

Euftis Emery

I'm Shy...

Aquino and Bridget finally came into the living room with Bridget sitting in the leather chair that mirrored mine grinning the whole time. "*Passed the test I guess*", I thought as a visibly nervous Aquino walked up to me. I was a bit disappointed to see her dressed conservatively in a waist length multi-colored, turtleneck sweater, faded bell bottom jeans and a pair of canvas Chucks. Her hair, nails and makeup were as fierce as in her pictures. She looked cute, but I was expecting her to look sexier.

But being a good date, I didn't express my disappointment and flashed a warm smile at her. "Hi Euftis", she said in a quiet voice placing a hand on the left armrest of my chair and leaning to the side. She exhaled loudly and my eyes stayed locked on her ample chest as her large breasts moved down and up in her sweater.

It appeared that she was going to continue her conversation with me when she glanced over at her daughter struggling to set-up her hands free. "You got it working London", she asked her daughter.

London shook her hear saying no. "Euftis can you set it up for her", Aquino asked.

"I can try", I replied.

"Let Mr. Euftis fix it", Aquino told her daughter as she walked over to her taking the phone and headset giving both to me and then walked back into the kitchen with her best friend.

I assumed that she was talking about me again and while wondering just what she was saying I set to the task of

Euftis Emery

I'm Shy...

matching her daughter's headset with her phone. After ten minutes I figured it out and returned the items to London. She called her voicemail testing the connection. "Thank you...", she said simply looking at me for the first time and giving me a small smile.

Aquino came back into the living room ten minutes later wearing a parka and I got up assuming that she was ready to leave. "Did he fix it for you", Aquino asked her daughter who was busy talking on her phone. She shook her head in the affirmative looking over at me smiling.

"Thank you Euftis", Aquino told me honestly. "I can't figure out technical stuff like that I appreciate your help."

With that statement she became five times more attractive to me. It was obvious that she was accustomed but more importantly...appreciated...having a man around and a woman who freely respected a man's role in the home was well worth having.

"You're welcome", I replied standing up assuming that she was ready to leave. "You ready to go?"

"I'm gonna go to dinner with Mr. Euftis guys", Aquino said to her children. Her daughter looked up and glanced at both of us with the same slight smile she showed me earlier, but her brother continued to pretend that I didn't exist, as he stayed transfixed to his game.

We walked out of the house into the driveway and I asked Aquino if she would drive. Whenever I go out of town to visit a female, I ask them if they will drive. After all, I made the effort to come and see them the least that a woman can

Euftis Emery

do is drive in a town that I'm unfamiliar with. A woman who would make an issue of this may be too selfish to be bothered with, but I was again pleasantly surprised when she had no problem pulling out her keys after I explained my rationale.

We climbed into her truck and proceeded to The Greene in Beaver Creek, Ohio on the outskirts of Dayton. The drive was unusually quiet with Aquino appearing nervous. I probed Aquino's background to attempt to break the ice. "So, what do you do for a living?"

"I teach kindergarten students at Bloom Elementary", she replied timidly.

I giggled inwardly. "A freak kindergarten schoolteacher", I thought. "A stay at home mom's nightmare. I bet allot of mother's hate on her for taking their husbands attention during parent teachers conferences."

"So does your kids Dad spend time with them", I asked continuing to probe into Aquino's background.

"My husband was killed", Aquino replied simply. That let me know that there wasn't any baby Daddy or psycho ex issues to deal with but based on the seriousness of her answer I wished that I could take back the question.

"He really took care of me", Aquino continued. "But he also sheltered me. There's so much that I don't know about that I want to experience. That's why I set-up my profile the way I did on BP. I'm enjoying the reactions guys are having over me wearing things that my husband would never let me wear."

I'm Shy…

Aquino's confession confirmed that she was a freak. Albeit one that just burst forth from her cocoon. Her phone had been ringing continuously once we got in her truck and it was beginning to get on my nerves. It's all-good if you're a player or playette but it's not when you make it obvious. Basic dating etiquette is to always give the appearance that you're not a player.

Truth be told, my phone had gone off a few times as well, but I kept my phone on vibrate and in my pocket. So as far as Aquino knew my attention was all on her. And I expected the same courtesy. Her phone rang again, and I flicked my eyes at it flaring for several seconds. Aquino got the hint, put the phone on vibrate and stuck it in her purse.

We got to The Greene, parked the car and went into the Cheesecake factory. It was busy   but we didn't have to wait long for a seat. They seated us in the rear of the restaurant in a booth and I flashed the pearly whites and struck a handsome pose at my date.

Aquino reacted by turning to the side in her seat. Her hair obscured the majority of her face and she rested her face on her cheek covering the rest. "What's…up…", I asked amused.

"You're staring at me. I'm…shy…", Aquino replied talking in her hand.

"*Shy*…", I thought. "Stop playing Aquino. Turn around and talk to me."

Aquino turned around facing me for several seconds and then turned to the side again giving me another close-up view of her hair.

Euftis Emery

I'm Shy…

I was initially amused with Aquino's behavior and momentarily distracted when the waitress came and took our order. I ordered a top shelf long island with Jamaican chicken and shrimp while Aquino (still hiding her face from me) ordered a house salad with pink lemonade.

"What's...up...", I asked Aquino again prompting her to hide even more giving me a view of nothing but blond hair. "Are you for real", I demanded incredulously.

"I'm...shhhhhhhhhy...", Aquino whined.

Getting no entertainment from my date, I turned my attention to the other tables to do some people watching. The table across from me gained my immediate interest.

Three couples where having dinner together and they were all very attractive black folk. But what captured my attention was that they all had the latest Blackberry and they were all busy setting them up. The glimpses of the colorful screens that I caught had me transfixed like a woman looking at diamonds in a jewelry store.

I wanted to get and look over one of their shoulders to get a feel for the device but didn't because I knew none of them would have been comfortable with that. I was determined to get an iPhone and although the Blackberry looked interesting soon, I lost interest and turned back to my date.

"You still on that...I'm shy...shit", I asked Aquino not getting a response. She was still turned to the side hiding her face with her hair and hand.

Euftis Emery

I'm Shy...

"You know what Eddie Murphy says about women over thirty talking about...they shy", I continued. "I'm gonna give you ten seconds to get off that shit. If you don't, there won't be any desert or movie. I'm gonna take you home and show you what I do to...shy...girls."

Aquino turned to face me slowly and looked at me with large, fear filled eyes.

"You wanna know what I do to shy girls", I continued. "I fuck 'em in the ass! No hugging. No kissing. Just str8 ass fucking. Do you want to get fucked in the ass tonight?"

Aquino's eyes became even wider and she even had the nerves to blush then she turned to the side again hiding her face with her hair.

"*Yea...that's what I thought. You ain't a stranger to having a dick all up in your ass*", I thought noting that my date didn't make one squeak of protest after me telling her that I planned on having anal sex with her.

"Alright. You were warned", I continued fatalistically. Soon as we get done with our meal, I'm taking you home and....fucking you in your ass."

****

We ate dinner in relative silence and then I escorted Aquino back to her truck with a hand firmly clasped around her right bicep to emphasize to her that I meant business. We got into her vehicle and she looked at me with timid eyes non-verbally asking...*where are we going.*

Euftis Emery

I'm Shy…

"We're going back to your house", was my stern reply to her non-verbal question and I pointed in the general direction for emphasis.

We got back to her house and when we walked in the door, we found her kids fast asleep on the couch with the lights on and television blaring. Bridget was nowhere to be found and I assumed that she went home.

Aquino looked as if she was confused with what she should do next as she looked back and forth from her children and me. "Bedroom...", I asked simply.

Girlfriend blushed again looking at me wide-eyed and conflicted. I went str8 pimp on her and gave her a hard look that said the only thing that needed to come out of her mouth was the direction to her bedroom.

"Up the stairs...first room on the right", Aquino replied getting the message giving me a small, nervous smile.

Acting like I lived there, I went upstairs to Aquino's spacious bedroom. The first thing that I noticed in her room was the huge brass bed that I had seen in her pictures. It dominated the room imposingly and was decorated with a patterned brown leather comforter. "*Sista got good taste*", I thought approvingly.

The next thing that I noticed in her room were framed...nude...pictures of Aquino decorating the room. "*Shy my ass*", I thought amused. "*You're not that shy if you would frame glamour freak shots within access of your own kids.*"

Still smiling, I took off my jacket and draped it over her desk

Euftis Emery

I'm Shy...

chair. "*It's gonna be...on.. all....night...long...in this bitch*", I thought gleefully.

That second Aquino walked into the room looking nervous. I smiled at her broadly and she walked halfway towards me. She left the door open and stared at me silently and I stared back looking at her non-verbally saying...*what's up?*

Aquino walked back to the door and closed it leaving a small crack open. She then turned towards me and stared again.

Without comment, I strode forward, reached around her and closed her bedroom door. I then pushed in the lock smartly making no attempt to do it quietly. Aquino exhaled quietly accepting her fate and placing my hands on her shoulder I sat her down on her king-sized bed.

I sat down beside her and before I could get to waxing that ass...literally...first I had to query Aquino about her glamour freak pictures. "I'm scared of your pictures baby. Where did you take that one", I asked pointing at the picture that sat next to her bed? In the picture she was sitting on a stool cupping her juicy DD's in her hands holding them up to some lucky, unseen photographer. She was wearing some kind of black leather harness. I won't call it an outfit because there was only a one-inch strip of leather that came around her neck and wrapped around the base of her breasts and then ran down the center of her chest over her belly button. I longed to see the rest of her...outfit...from front to back.

"Ohhhhh...I took that at the school", Aquino replied casually.

My mouth dropped open before I could catch it but Aquino didn't notice. I wanted to ask her some additional questions

Euftis Emery

I'm Shy…

like how she explained the pictures to her children, relatives
and friends when they came into her room but I was so
floored with her telling me that she took one of the pictures
at the elementary school where she taught that I decided it
would be best if I left any further questions alone.

After shaking my head wondering what else Ms. Shy was into,
I grasped the bottom of her turtleneck with both hands and
slowly lifted it over her head. She blushed and looked pitiful
again, but I totally ignored her so-called silent protest and
stared hard at her bra-encased breasts. "Stand up", I
demanded as I continued to strip Aquino down.

She of course did as she was told, and I took my time pealing
her out of her jeans. After I got her out of the bulk of her
clothing, I noticed that her smooth, light skin was tatted up.

I took inventory of each one of them, slowly tracing around
each one of them with my index finger. Starting with the
tiger on her right ankle, moving to the heart on her hip, lazily
drifting to the mask on her left thigh, dwelling a while with
the rose on her left breast, ending with the band adorned
with three hearts on her left arm.

Aquino intently watched as I traced each of her tattoo's
enjoying the eroticism. It was a sweet moment, but I had a
promise to keep. "Sit on the floor", I commanded.

"Sit... On the floor...", Aquino asked confused.

"Yes. Sit... On the floor", I replied.

Aquino sat on the floor with her back to the side of her bed
and looked up at me curiously. She didn't have long to

Euftis Emery

wonder why because I immediately unzipped my pants and put dick all in her face.

She didn't open her mouth quick enough for me, so I reached to the back of her head and took a handful of her hair pulling head back roughly. She gave me the response I wanted by opening her mouth in shock and as soon as she did semi-hard dick slid into her mouth.

"Ohhhhhhh...yeaaaaaa...", I groaned looking up at the ceiling as Aquino moaned and sucked me slowly savoring how I grew within her mouth with each passing second.

"Not acting shy now are you", I asked mischievously as I pulled Sergio out of her mouth and slapped her right cheek with my dick and then rubbed the tip of it on her lips teasingly.

"Baaaaabe...", Aquino cooed as the head of my penis rubbed against her bottom lip.

Pulling her head back again by her hair. Knowing what I wanted she opened her mouth wide and looked up at me with wide, beseeching eyes. I granted her request willing and buried now hard dick down the length of her tongue and pressed against her tonsils.

Aquino gagged, placing her right hand around my shaft and left hand on my thigh as she pressed back against both. "Put your hands down", I snapped loudly, and Aquino complied placing her hands palms down on the floor.

Pulling her head back by her hair repositioned my shaft in her mouth so that I was no longer pressing against her tonsils and

I'm Shy…

I milked Sergio with my free hand giving Aquino my sweet and yet salty taste. "Ohhhhhh...I...like...you...", I purred as she slurped my delicious juices with fluttering eyes.

"Now...*get*...it...", I commanded releasing her hair now that I knew that she would obey and give me everything that I wanted.

I told her to get it and she got it. Grasping my member with both hand and sucking with quick, vigorous head movements as if it would be her last time. "But your damn hands down", I demanded as Aquino quickly placed her hands back on the floor.

"Pick 'em back up", I said changing my mind. "Pull those big titties out!"

Aquino reached up and roughly pulled the cups of her bra under her breasts releasing them. Upon doing that, her hands wavered a bit as she tried to figure out what to do with them.

Her right nipple was pierced, and I pulled on the ring a bit teasing it. "Why didn't you pierce the other one", I asked.

"I planned to. But it hurt so...baaaad...when I did the first one, I was too scared to do the other one", she replied meekly.

"Well put your hands back down and open your mouth wide", I demanded after I stopped playing with her breast. "I want to fuck your mouth."

Aquino complied and I put both hands in her hair to control her head as I slow stroked her mouth. She swallowed

Euftis Emery

I'm Shy...

infrequently as my pre-cum leakage filled the back of her throat and I grinned broadly each time she did. I love that shit. I love feeding a woman my essence and watching her take my D.N.A. into her body binding a part of me into her. My statement may appear a bit twisted to some of you reading this, but I do. I...love...it...

I continued to mouth fuck her slowly until I couldn't take it any longer and I pulled out before I busted in her mouth. Don't get me wrong...I...planned...on busting in her mouth. Just at a later date.

"Get on your knees on the bed", I told Aquino ready to take things up a notch.

She climbed up on the bed fetchingly and looked back at me over her left shoulder expectantly. I pulled down her yellow thong until I could see her chocolate starfish and golden triangle. Both of them were gaping and inviting and I wasted no time In saying hello by putting my tongue into the starfish.

"Ohhhhhh...baaaaabe...", Aquino purred as I enjoyed myself liking her ass. Aquino loved the tongue down that I was giving her anus, but she fought with her feelings to prevent making too much noise.

But I wanted her ass ready for the fucking I planned on giving it. Using both hands I spread her cheeks as far as I could and buried my tongue deep in her anus.

"Babe... Baaaaabe...wait...", Aquino protested.

"*Slap*...", was my response as I popped her with a good over hand smack on her right butt cheek. The smack reverberated

Euftis Emery

in her room and her back arched wonderfully in surprise.

"Baaabe… I don't want my kids to hear.", Aquino whined.

"*Slap… Slap*", was my reply as I gave her right cheek another good overhand smack and then whipped an even harder cross slap on her left cheek before the sound of the first slap could subside.

"Ohhh… Ohhhhhhhhhhhh...c'mon babe...", Aquino whimpered jiggling her ass a bit in an effort to relieve the sting. Her actions turned me on even more because her protests were weak denoting that she really liked it. Her high yella rump was marred with red marks where my hand made contact with it and I smiled broadly appreciating my handiwork. I love spanking ass too. Especially on a redbone that liked it.

After showing Aquino that I was the one running shit, I spread her cheeks again and commenced deep fucking her anus with my tongue. On each plunge into her rectal depths I got at least four inches of tongue.

Pushed over the brink, Aquino's voice went up in volume as she lost her self-control. "*Babe! Babe! Babe! Babe*", she crooned in a high falsetto each time my tongue penetrated past the ring of her sphincter muscle.

I continued tongue fucking her ass gathering saliva on the tip of my tongue before each plunge getting her rectum nice and lubricated. The best ass fucking is done with natural lubricants. Saliva, girl juice, pre-cum and cum. A real bitch takes the dick in the ass that way and leaves the manufactured stuff in the store.

Euftis Emery

I'm Shy...

So, I continued my assault until the booty was juicy and loose. Then I let my tongue slide down her crack until I hit her taint. I sucked that a bit teasing her and then licked slowly around her inner lips to sample her taste. She was delectable.

After passing my taste test I inhaled deeply with my nose hovering a few inches from her opening and then plunged my tongue to the root exploring the inner recesses of her other opening.

"*Ohhhhhhhhh.... Babe! Ohhhhhhhhh... Babe*", Aquino sang even louder enjoying my oral ministration.

I detailed her pussy and then dropped down to her engorged clit and put a rhythm on it, sucking it hard three times and then flicking the tip of my tongue on it for five.
"Ohhhhhhh... Damn! Baaaaabe! Damn! Baaaaabe", she carried on giving it up.

"Ahhhhhhhh...yea bitch", I thought. "It's gonna be on up in her tonight! If you didn't know you know now!"

I sucked and licked. Licked and sucked until my jaws hurt and then it was time to give Aquino what I promised. Standing up, I took her by the hips and pulled her closer to the edge of the bed and then pressed the head of my dick against her rectal opening.

Aquino didn't fuse or complain. She just waited patiently for me to stick it in, so I did. Pushing slowly, I got my head past the only point of resistance...the sphincter muscle and then I waited.

Euftis Emery

I'm Shy…

I planned on just staying like that for several minutes giving Aquino time to relax but she started clenching the dick with her rectum signaling that she wanted more so I gave it to her.

I dug deeper and Aquino thrilled me to no end when she responded by lowing her head so I could get even deeper, so I did. "*Ohhhhhhh… Damn! Baaaaabe! Damn! Baaaaabe*", girlfriend carried on as I continued to get it all in.

"Like that don't you", I said as I began to talk shit. Taking another handful of hair, I pulled it back until I buried myself in her to the root.

"Told you I was gonna get that ass didn't I", I whispered with my lips to her ear.

Aquino didn't reply but turned her head and tried to kiss me. "Uhhhh uhh… There'll be no hugging or kissing tonight. Just str8 ass fucking", I said evilly as I moved my head back before our lips made contact.

"You ready for me to…fuck it…", I asked putting my lips back to her ear. "Huh? You ready for me to get this ass?"

"Yes babe! Fuck it! Fuck my ass", Aquino exclaimed loudly.

With her willing consent (in all seriousness I would have took it anyway) I began to beat the ass up with…long…hard…strokes. I got ten good stokes in when Aquino ran from the dick by laying down flat on the bed. I followed her down to the bed as she ran not letting Sergio slip out of her anus.

72

Euftis Emery

I'm Shy...

"Look at you...trying to run", I said laying on top of her as I continued to pound it.

"Ohhhhhhh...babe... Not so loud. Please babe... I don't want my kids to hear this", Aquino begged.

"You...got...nerves... Telling me.... To be quiet... After all the yelling you been doing", I replied amused.

I continued to put work in and Aquino lost control again and whimpered, moaned, and coaxed at the top of her lungs.

The ass fucking continued fast and furiously for another twenty minutes and then I busted a huge load in Aquino's rectum. She took it like a champ and when my body stopped spasming I rolled off her to find her smiling.

"Are you gonna spend the night with me", Aquino asked sweetly.

"Nawwww...I'm gonna make that run and head home in a minute", I replied.

"I...hate..that shit", Aquino exclaimed angrily. "I hate it when a guy just hits it and leaves!"

"Hold on. Now hold on baby", I replied as I explained myself. "I...would...spend the night and I want to. But my girls are at home alone. So, I can't stay the night."

Upon receiving my explanation, Aquino visibly relaxed. "Alright then. I understand."

"Good. I didn't want you thinking that I just wanted to do a

Euftis Emery

I'm Shy...

hit and run", I replied digging that Aquino wanted intimacy in addition to sex from me.

A mischievous grin formed on Aquino's face as she rolled over onto her stomach and looked back at me. "Well before you go why don't you hit this ass one more time."

I smiled. *"God...I love shy girls"*, I thought.

Euftis Emery

I'm Shy...

Euftis currently resides in Cincinnati, Ohio. He is a graduate of Howard University with a degree in Computer Based Information Systems. Founding Dominion Publishing in 2005, Euftis has quickly become one of the most daring and raw black erotic authors on the market today.

Euftis can be reached at Euftis_Emery@

Euftis Emery

I'm Shy...

Euftis Emery